PARK LIFE

BY

LYNN McLEAN

The intense June sun coming in from all the windows that made up the conservatory, was making Tina Henderson feel very sleepy and relaxed. A glance at the wall clock showed her it was close to 3pm, retired now for 5years, she was enjoying all the benefits of a more benign lifestyle. Free now from all the hassle n stress of early mornings, boring meetings and sparse amounts of quality time to do the things she longed to do. Tina now had all the hours in a day to do whatever she felt like doing, which was in reality not that much really, lacking energy since retirement, doing her household chores of cleaning and laundry, and all the other bits of attention a home needs, well, it left her with just wanting to catch up with the latest on her soaps and general interest programmes. Like escape to the country, and The Chase.

Plus, she and her husband were now carrying a tad extra bit weight than they did when they were both still employed. The more sedate lifestyle, and eating far more than they usually would, they had each steadily climbed up the scales, it didn't bother her at first, but now she felt frumpy, the clothes she liked no longer looked as good as they should on her now larger 5ft 2inch frame. John had recently been told he had type 2 diabetes, time for change she thought, no more rich sauces etc.. except for special occasions.

John, her husband, had just popped out to mail a birthday card to their grandson Jack, the usual gift of money was enclosed. They had decided a few years back to now just gift money on birthdays. The grandchildren were all over 15 years of age and they had no clue really on the kinds of things teenagers would appreciate, so a monetary gift to spend on what they actually wanted seemed the sensible thing to do from then on.

Tina was just beginning to doze off when a scratching sound disturbed her. As she looked through towards the kitchen where the sound was emanating from, she saw their dog Alfie, he was not so patiently wagging his tail and looking expectantly at the back door. A sweet fluffy brown and white shitzu they had adopted from a local shelter four years ago. Alfie was a welcome addition to their home. John had been wanting a dog for years, but with them both working, it was a little pipe dream that was now reality. Tina, although a bit apprehensive at first, now had as much love for the little ball of fur as John did.

"ok Alfie, mummy's coming" Tina said as she eased herself from the armchair and made her way from the conservatory to through the kitchen.

On seeing her come towards him, Alfie started wagging his tail with such vigour it was just a blur. The closer Tina got, Alfie started barking and he did what they referred to as the "poo" dance, bouncing on his two front paws until the door was opened.

Darting outside Alfie began sniffing frantically and danced around in circles till he found that magic spot to do his business.

Just at that time when Alfie was relieving himself, john arrived home and opened the front door, Tina quickly grabbed the handle of the internal kitchen door to stop it slamming with the through draft.

"quickly John, get in, I have just let the dog out and the back door is open, he is leaving you a little present on the grass" she chuckled, letting go of the door handle as her husband closed the front door.

"I tell ye what Tina, there are some right arseholes on the road today, some twat in a BMW, no consideration or care for anyone, just cut me up at the roundabout coming back into Carnegie Avenue, then just as I was turning off for Dovecot I had to slam on my brakes for one of those braindead Skye workers over taking, I tell ye, they won't be so cocky when they wrap their car round a tree" , said a very irate John as he fished a doggy poo bag out his jacket pocket.

"why do you always blame Skye workers dear ?, it could well have been anyone" answered Tina, as John made his way outside and bent to remove Alfie's little deposit.

He stood back up and said "because it's the back of 4oclock, ye know how crazy they get, too much of a hurry to get home before the traffic gets heavy" john grumbled as he tied a knot in the little grey bag as he placed it in the blue landfill bin. He then came inside and made his way to the downstairs bathroom to wash his hands, still grumbling under his breath about idiots behind the wheel.

Tina rolled her eyes and knew just to drop the subject or he would just keep moaning, she shut the back door after getting Alfie back inside and called out down the hall

"I fancy getting a Camdean takeaway for tea tonight, what do you think John? I really don't fancy cooking as its too hot, we could perhaps take the dog for a walk in the Glen first, and wait till the sun goes down a bit before ordering"

"Actually that's a really good idea Tina, I have been craving his beef curry lately" smiled John, all thought of bad drivers forgotten as he walked back into the kitchen.

"Great, it's still a bit early, and now that I don't have to prepare anything, you can help me see to the garden plants, cup of tea first though before we get cracking on it, then have a nice wee stroll round the Glen with the mutt" smiled Tina as she flicked the kettle on. Trying hard not to notice John rolling his eyes behind her back. He had no idea that she could see his reflection in the window beside where the kettle was. John hated gardening, but she needed his help digging small holes for the bedding plants.

Two hours later and they were both satisfied with how the garden was looking, the colours of the varying flowers went well with where they had been placed. The patio roses that ran along the low wall beside the steps that led to their small summer house, were especially vibrant and full of blooms, Tina though, thought that the many coloured petunia would have to be cut back a little, they were growing like weeds.

June was turning out to be just as hot and dry as May had been, which was a rarity as locals always joked about the "2 days of summer", the weather was, more often than not dull and wet or at the very least just cloudy.

Having given the plants a good generous amount of water, they both stood back, near their French doors and admired their evenings work

"I think we will get a hose pipe ban if this keeps up" said John."

"it really would not surprise me if that happened, look at how the grass is starting to go brown, and I don't mean where Alfie has peed" laughed Tina

"maybe we should pop to Dobbies tomorrow and get one of those sprinklers Dave next door has, shame the look of the garden could be ruined just because of a wee bit brown grass" answered John as he turned and looked at his wife expectantly, waiting on an answer.

"knowing our luck it will rain the day after we buy the damn thing, Fife as you know never gets weather this nice, but we could go....just for a look mind, and no, you do not need a new mower or strimmer or any other tool" replied Tina, giving her husband a look of mock stern as John stood there grinning.

"ok, ok, I am going to have a quick shower and get changed before we go our walk, I'm feeling really sticky and dirty, especially after digging in muck" he said as he stood with his hands up in surrender.

"I need a shower too, mind if I join you" Tina replied, trying her hardest not to laugh.

"steady on woman, I am an old man who has just about enough energy to amble around the park. Perhaps you will get lucky later tonight" winked John as he started to go indoors.

Tina sighed and smiled to herself, no chance she thought. By 10pm we will both be asleep in our chairs.

Now almost 7.30pm, Tina had snapped Alfies lead onto his collar and was making her way to the front door, a very excited Alfie was crying and bouncing around in circles, coming precariously close to being stood on numerous times.

"Tina, where the Hell did I leave my keys, bloody sure the damn things sprout legs" shouted John from upstairs. Tina rolled her eyes n shook her head, this was not a rare occurrence, John was forever losing his keys, putting them down wherever and never remembering, she had tried to get him into the habit of placing them in the bowl that was on the kitchen table, but gave up and put it down to wasted breath trying to get him to comply with what she kept telling him was common sense.

"try looking on top of the bedside cabinet on your side dear, or even in the bathroom, failing that, check your trouser pockets" replied Tina, as she held onto the bottom part of the bannister looking expectantly up the stairs, cocking her head waiting for a reply.

"found them" replied John, Tina smiled to herself and turned to Alfie and said "what on earth would that man do without me Alfie eh?" Alfie had stopped bouncing around and was looking at Tina with expectation, not really sure why he had his lead on and was not going anywhere. That excitement was reignited on seeing his master start to come down the stairs. "right then woman and mutt, lets be off" grinned John.

With Alfie safely secured in the back seat of their new sleek black Range Rover, that John assured everyone was "sex on wheels", they reversed out of the driveway and made their way to Queensferry Road at the bottom of their housing estate, to join onto duel traffic on the way to Dunfermline.

"where shall we park this time, near the pavilion, Carnegie birthplace, or see if there are any spaces over from that Lorenzos place" said Tina turning to look at John, he was the one driving but it was always Tina who decided, but she liked John to think she valued his opinion in the matter.

"wherever you think is best honey" replied John, Tina just smiled, nodded her head and said,

"lets try across from that Lorenzos, its nice and close to the Abbey, and it is looking absolutely gorgeous just now with all the summer flowers and plants" John gave a slight nod of his head in answer, and the rest of the short journey was done in silence as Tina gazed out of the slightly rolled down window, looking at the laburnum trees and other walkers out enjoying the remains of the day. Tina smiled at the antics of a group of young children, chasing each other with water guns, screaming in delight if they got soaked, in the distance she could make out the sound of an ice cream van as it did it's rounds. He will be busy selling ice cream and lollies today she thought.

Soon they arrived at their chosen site for parking, Alfie sensing that freedom was imminent went into a little whimpering frenzy, his tail just a blur of excitement and his small body frantically trying to escape the confinement of his pet seatbelt restraint.

"would you listen to the state of him" remarked John as he turned off the engine, making sure his wing mirrors were tucked in, because you could never be too careful with all the idiots that had no respect for anyone else's vehicles. Tina knew John had a touch of paranoia regarding other road users, especially since getting this new car. But she also knew that John was far from being a perfect driver himself. He was frequently using any lane he felt like, regardless if it was the right one, he drove too fast at times too and sometimes he didn't even use his indicators.

"really dear, it should not be a surprise as he does this every time" laughed Tina, she already had her door open and was removing Alfie's lead from her cardigan pocket. After closing her door and opening the rear passenger side, she opened it just enough to grab the dogs collar for clipping his lead on.

They learnt the hard way that Alfie just got too excited for liberation, and he would just bolt out the door if given the chance. It had taken them over an hour one time, when he has slipped Johns clutches to get him back, and that was only because Alfie was such a friendly dog and had run up to another walker, also with a shitzu, Alfie desperate to play had bounded in the other dog's direction. The owner of the other dog had been happy to grab Alfies collar to aid in his capture. John had put his back out during that incident, Alfie had seen it as a game and kept darting off whenever john got close enough to bend and grab him, Tina could not risk that happening again, John was a big moaning baby when he wasn't fighting fit.

With Alfies lead now firmly on and secure, they locked the car up and stated to walk down the side steps of the lower carpark, Alfie pulling on his lead in an effort to make them go faster. In doing so, he always ended up coughing a bit with the collar digging into his neck.

"I really wish he wouldn't do that, you would think at least one of his brain cells would tell him its futile" said Tina.

"well at least he only does it initially, he does calm down soon enough, damn embarrassing though" answered John, making clucking noises as he took the lead from his wife.

 Alfie may be a wee dog, but he had some strength in him when he pulled on the lead, which Tina struggled with. John would hand her the control back when Alfie had calmed down a bit.

The trio walked on past the side of the Abbey, where some of Scotlands medieval monarchs had been laid to rest, the Abbey had initially been founded as a priory by David I or Dauid mac Mail Choluim, the youngest son of MalcolmIII, and was later to become a royal mausoleum.

The Abbey has been a site of Christian worship for over a thousand years, John especially thought it was one of the most beautiful buildings Scotland had, even though he was not a church goer, he particularly loved the Romanesque architecture which made up the old building. He was proud to be born and bred in Dunfermline.

They walked on past the old ruins on the left hand side, reminiscing about when they were younger and were able to play there, pretending they were Kings and Queens as they darted about the ancient ruined halls.

People could only have access now by tour, which was just as well, too many vandals and it really was not a place for unsupervised children, they marvelled at how they were still alive at some of the risks they had taken whilst playing there. That of course led onto them talking about all the things The Glen no longer had. The maze, the paddling pools, which were so busy back when they were kids, so popular, it seemed like every family in the area came there on warm sunny days, the bike park, which was made up of little child size roads, not forgetting the animal area, which was Tina's favourite place, full of monkeys, snakes, birds etc, she loved the big owl and then running down to the bunny house which was a segmented cage you could walk round, looking at all the different rabbits.

Sadly, that was all gone now, but the hothouse was still there, as was the museum and the pavilion, and there was an amazing park for the children to play in. also the peacock café which served some great cakes and tea and coffee. The Glen was a very beautiful place to have a walk around, full of colour, little nooks and crannies to explore, amazing trees and the squirrels, lots n lots of squirrels.

After John and Tina had entered the park gates, Tina pressed the little switch on the handle of Alfies lead, this released a longer length which was encased in the handle , so Alfie could feel free to sniff and explore, but without him being able to disappear if he happened to spot a squirrel that needed to be chased.

"I think we should head down past the hothouse to the bottom field, let the dog spend some of that pent up energy, then up past the pavilion to the top gates, then a nice wee stroll through the bottom paths back to the car, or is that too much for an old man" smirked Tina, as she looked up into her husband's face, waiting on his reaction to being called old.

"enough of the old, I can still run rings round the snowflake youth of today, I have plenty stamina, which I will prove later tonight" he smiled while giving her a sideways glance.

The five friends were getting bored and itching for something to do, other than hanging around Queen Anne Street at the back of Dunfermline bus station.

They had already been moved on by security twice today so far, because of threatening unruly behaviour, with the added promise that the police would be called if they showed face again.

Dylan the oldest of the group at 19 years old, all the rest being 18, was in the process of taking a long puff on the joint he had just made, tall at 6 foot, slim built with dark greasy hair and wearing an Adidas tracksuit that he got on knock off, he cared not a bit that he was blatantly smoking an illegal substance in the presence of passers by, totally oblivious to the looks of disapproval, and the wide berth the group in general were getting from the general public.

"come on, pass it you greedy cunt" said Neil, looking up at Dylan while snapping his fingers and reaching out.

"click your fingers at me one more time mate, n I will break the fuckers" replied Dylan, blowing out the pungent smelling smoke towards the other boys face.

"ladies first anyway, I put in more money than you" said Gwen, an attractive girl with her long straightened bleach blonde hair, and vibrant green eyes which were too heavily made up and always had mascara goop in the corner, wearing skinny fit jeans and dark purple hoodie.

"fuck off, you only put in more coz Hannah gave you money to put towards it" replied Neil

"so fucking what dickhead, we still put more in than you" said Hannah, sneering at him and waiting for an argument. Although plainer looking than Gwen, she was still attractive, wearing almost identical clothes to her friend, she had dark blonde hair and wore no makeup.

"aww stuff this man, can we not go somewhere else? Some cunt is bound to grass us up for having a doobie, and plod are up n down here aww the time, we don't want them finding out it was us that gave those boys a kicking last week. Plus, its boring as fuck here" interrupted Danny.

Danny was unpredictable. Anything could set off his violence and it usually did, no matter how small. At only 5ft 7 there were those who underestimated his level of violence because of his short stature. Like the two men who they attacked last week.

 It all started because Danny was in a mood of unknown reason, it was late on a Thursday night, roughly 11.30pm. the group were hanging around on the stairs leading down from Bruce

Street, which led down to the City Hotel carpark, when two men, roughly in their 30's came down the steps. Danny insisted that one of the men looked at him as if he was shit, and then he had stood in front of the two men demanding they apologise. The men didn't, and went to walk past.

That was when Danny lost it. He punched the first one so hard he was knocked out straight away. The second man barely had time to register what had happened before Danny swung for him too, but it was a glancing punch. This sent Danny into a rage, he grabbed the man by his shirt front, pulled him forward and headbutted him in the face, blood instantly exploded everywhere but the man was trying to fight back. This was when the rest of the group joined in.

The girls, Gwen and Hannah started kicking and stomping on the prone knocked out individual, while the three boys laid into the other, whose nose, Danny had surely broken. It wasn't long before both men were now unconscious on the steps, covered in blood and torn clothes. A strong smell of copper hung in the air from the amount of blood, which mixed with the faint aroma of nearby takeaway places and the hint of stale urine that clung to those steps, the smell ingrained after many a drunk relieving themselves over the years. .

The whole attack took less than 3 minutes.

The group fled the scene after a last kick from Danny, straight in the face to the first man who had started moaning as he lay there, the sound of bone crunching as his cheek folded in was audible and sickening, They ran away down the rest of the steps and on through the city carpark, up past the 7 Kings pub on the corner, and then straight over the road and through the Glen gates, all the while laughing about how the guy had pissed himself while lying there.

"hey, why don't we go a wee wander back in the glen, beats hanging here doing fuck all" suggested Gwen, bringing their thoughts back to the present. looking at the faces of her friends waiting on their response.

"fuck it, let's go, I just can't stand being here any longer" replied Danny, standing up, he snorted loudly then spat a glob of phlegm onto the bench where he had been sitting. He started to walk away not waiting to see or even care if his friends followed, he knew they would though.

Danny started walking down the little path that went through a small grass area that connected the high street to Queen Anne Street.

The town centre was getting quieter now, most shoppers had already made their way home, shop and business workers were walking with a bit more speed than the average shopping straggler, eager to get home and hopefully enjoy relaxing in what was left of such a lovely hot day, after being cooped inside at work all day.

Like sheep, the rest of the group all followed, Neil and Dylan catching up to Danny and walking either side of him, Gwen and Hannah bringing up the rear a few paces back from the boys. No one spoke; they walked a short distance down the hill before coming to the junction of Bruce street, Danny decided to cut across the road and walk past the city chambers building and down towards the Abbey, glancing in the window of The Creepy bar as he walked past, kind of hoping he would see his mate Tam, mainly because Tam was good for tapping a few quid off. He was not in luck tonight though.

Soon they had passed Life nightclub and were walking through the entrance of The Glen, directly opposite from the Abbeys main doors. The same entrance John and Tina Henderson had gone through just 20 minutes before them.

John and Tina had made it around to the front of Pittencrieff House, A 17th century building, bought by Andrew Carnegie in 1903. The house as well as the park, were given to the people of Dunfermline by Andrew Carnegie, and is now looked after by Fife council. The house is now a museum, exhibiting the park itself and Dunfermline town.

Both John and Tina had been eager to make it to the large grassed area in front of the House. Alfie had been kept on his leash until now, he was a good dog, but the temptation of chasing the numerous squirrels as they had entered The Glen, was way too much to ask for to expect Alfie to remain obedient, especially since the squirrels congregated at the double arch bridge, which was just a few minutes into the park, a favourite spot for people to feed nuts to them and take photographs. So it was always busy with tempting furry activity.

"Right mutt, let's see how fast you can bring this back" said John. He had bought one of those ball throwing things from Pets at Home and was happy to try it out. Alfie was beyond excited, yipping and barking and bouncing around in circles like something demented, eager for his master to throw the ball so he could unleash all his pent up energy.

John placed the tennis ball in the cupped holder and swung the curved stick high behind his right shoulder, and quickly swung it forward up and over. The ball flew through the air, much harder and further than John had ever been able to do it freehand.

"would ye look at that Tina, why the Hell did I not buy one of these things years ago, look how far it's gone, didn't even hurt my shoulder throwing it" said John in amazement, hands on his hips as he looked on in wonder at how far the ball was going, and was still going with Alfie in hot pursuit.

 Alfie soon caught up with the ball but dropped it in his frenzy to get it, he soon chased it down and picked it up in his mouth again and was now speeding back in victory to where John and Tina stood laughing.

"A few more throws like that and as well as his walk, he is going to sleep for ages tonight, we can get to eat our takeaway in peace without the little moocher begging for a taste" remarked Tina, as she bent and clapped her hands on her knees in an effort to make Alfie return faster.

Alfie on returning, refused to hand over the slobber covered ball, he looked up at them with his forepaws on the ground and his tail wagging and rear end stuck up in the air, when John bent down to try and retrieve the toy, Alfie would go very still until Johns hand got too close then he would run a short distance away, and then stick his rear in the air again, waiting on John continuing the game. They both knew that Alfie would do this only for a short while before dropping the ball at their feet, and would get ready in a crouch position, eager to chase the ball after it had been thrown again.

They carried the game on as they walked past the gardens in front of the hothouse and followed the path down to the lower Glen gates, marvelling at the immense colour and diversity of the flora and fauna as they went. Tina stopping once in a while to smell a few flowers, not knowing the names of most of them, but kind of hoping they may have the same for sale at their favourite nursery, The Plant Market in Hillend near Dalgety Bay. She was not the greatest gardener, but she tried her best to have a bit colour in the garden. Most of the time her plants were ok, but some did die too, very much trial and error.

Alfie was now panting heavily with his large pink tongue flopping out the side of his mouth, but still wanting to play.

"I think we better stop and give the dog a little water dear, although the intense heat is gone, its still very hot n poor Alf is wearing a fur coat" advised Tina.

"aww Hell" replied John,

"I've only gone and forgot to lift his water bottle from the car, you should have reminded me Tina"   he said, feeling majorly guilty at having let poor Alfie down, especially since it was so warm.

"for goodness sake John, if I remind you, you have a go at me for nagging, and now that I didn't remind you its now all my fault because you forgot, I can't bloody win sometimes" Tina angrily responded, this was a major fault in John that really annoyed her more than anything else, the damn man found it near impossible to accept fault for almost everything he does wrongly, intended or not. Why the hell can he just not accept his shortcomings sometimes, plus it would stop the amount of little bickering fights they had on occasion, thought Tina.

"calm down woman, there's a little stream beside the bottom play park, we can just let him quench his thirst there, this once is not gonna kill him" grumbled John. He knew it was his fault, but hell would freeze over before he would admit it.

"hardly sanitary is it, gawd knows what's in that water" said Tina

"honey, he licks his arse n balls whenever he gets the chance, he is not going to be concerned about water from the burn is he?" remarked John, looking into his wife's face and hoping this was not going to turn into an argument after the evening being so pleasant.

Tina, not wanting to ruin the mood over something so trivial, sighed and gave her husband a sideways glance and a little smile.

"ok, I suppose you are right, but the sun is really starting to go down now, quick drink for Alfie then we better think about getting home and out of here before it gets too dark" she remarked .

Dylan, Neil and Danny are throwing stones from the double arch bridge, trying to see which one could hit a squirrel or pigeon first. Gwen and Hannah are sitting on the wall laughing at the unsuccessful attempts from the boys. Neil has come the closest to a direct hit, missing the little animal by an inch as it sat on the edge of the little summerhouse below the bridge.

"stupid furry little fuckers aint they? They keep coming back, probably think the stones are nuts or some fucking thing" laughed Danny, thoroughly enjoying himself as he threw another stone, which missed it's target yet again.

"hey, check out this wee bastard" shouted Neil. A small squirrel was just a few feet away hopping along the wall towards the group. Stopping every now and then to check it's surroundings, looking at the group of teens, hoping they may have food as so many people do when they come here. The squirrel showing curiosity rather than fear.

"one of us is bound to hit the little shit if we all throw at the same time, all of ye, get a stone and go on count of 3" grinned Danny as he turned to look at his friends. Dylan, Neil, Gwen and Hannah all picked up a stone and all pulled back their throwing arm in readiness for the launch.

"1, 2, 3" shouted Danny, as they all threw their stones at the same time. One stone hit the mark on the animals left side, it gave a squeak of distress but darted away quickly into the foliage seemingly unharmed.

"I got the wee cunt, ya beauty" cheered Dylan with his hands in the air, marching up and down the path ecstatic, a massive grin on his face in triumph.

"fuck off prick, that was clearly one o the rest o us, you threw too late ya knob" responded Danny, walking over to Dylan maliciously, standing pressing his chest against the other teen in an act of aggressive challenge, forcing the other boy to start walking backwards.

 Dylan did not want to argue or contest Danny, he knew the other boy would destroy him in a fight if he chose to stand up to him. Even though they were mates, Danny would not hesitate to start punching his older and taller friend.

"it's cool bro, I was only joking, I have no idea who hit the thing, just chuffed one of us got the cunt" replied the other boy, taking another step back and holding his hands palm up in an act of surrender, hoping it was enough to placate Danny's temper, and avoid an ugly kicking. Danny stared down the boy for a few seconds, then turned his back and went back to throwing stones. Immediately remorseful and thankful that it looked like Danny was not going to erupt, Dylan went and sat on the wall to the right of Hannah.

"well here's hoping it broke a bone or something and is going somewhere to die a slow agonising death" giggled Gwen, hanging onto the other girl's arm, they both started laughing at the thought.

"this is boring now anyway, there's fuck all to do here, we always do the same kind of shit every fucking night man, nothing exciting ever happens" said Neil as he lit a cigarette, which was immediately snatched out his mouth by Gwen. He just glowered at her, as he took the pack out his pocket and lit another.

A young couple pushing a buggy were passing the group, the little girl in the buggy not more than two years old. With the amount of foul language coming from the group, the young couple were giving them disapproving looks.

"The fuck you looking at mate" challenged Danny, walking towards them aggressively. Feet wide apart, his shoulders pulled back and chest pushed forward.

The young couple quickened their pace and said nothing, eager to leave the situation without conflict.

"that's right, keep fucking walking knob" Danny called after them. The couple looked back a few times before exiting up by the Abbey and turning the corner and were gone.

John and Tina were strolling back along the path that they had used to reach the little stream next to the playpark. Alfie now calm and energy spent, was walking calmly beside them. His tongue hanging out the side of his open panting mouth, drips of saliva frequently falling onto the dry parched ground.

The temperature had dropped even further and was now very comfortable, much better than the oppressive heat of the full sun. the sky was beginning to change colour to many shades of orange, red and pink. A perfect evening following a perfect day.

"isn't the Glen absolutely stunning against that sky, it seems to deepen the colours of the plants and flowers, kind of giving it a magical feel, don't you think John?" sighed Tina.

"it certainly is beautiful honey, so quiet too, I think we may be the last people in the park" answered John as he wrapped his arm around his wife's shoulders and kissed the top of her head.

"lets gets off home then, I'm getting peckish now, hopefully there will be a good film we can watch as we eat" smiled Tina, totally content.

They carried on walking up past the gardens and museum, watching the activity of round fluffy bees as the carried on visiting as many flowers as the could in the last minutes of sunlight, chatting about anything and everything and wondering when it would eventually rain, Alfie plodding along beside them, occasionally sniffing a bush and lifting his leg to mark his visit. The couple were just walking along the path that ran between the Museum and the pond, when Alfie ran ahead of them.

"ALFIE, " shouted John

"He probably spotted a squirrel, here John, take his lead and get it on him" advised Tina, passing her husband the lead after taking it out her cardigan pocket.

John walked just a little quicker around the corner onto the double arch bridge, in pursuit of their wayward dog. He stopped in his tracks to assess the situation when he saw a group of teenagers walking towards him. One of them was holding Alfie firmly under his arm. Alfie began to squirm to be set free.

"Thank you son, just put him down please, he is my dog, he will come right over to me" said John, feeling very uneasy, he didn't like the way the teens were staring at him, and they had stopped moving forward.

"did you get him dear" asked Tina, having caught up to her husband on turning the corner. She too stopped walking and just looked at Alfie in the teenage boys arms, she too felt uneasy. Mainly because they had heard so many bad stories of violence involving teenagers occurring in Dunfermline lately, but there was never any news about trouble from them in the Glen.

Tina gave herself a shake, they are just kids, doesn't mean they are bad kids she told herself.

"There you are you naughty ball of fur, thank you for grabbing him for us, I think he was chasing a squirrel, just put him down love, he will come to us" said Tina to the boy, giving him and the rest of the group a friendly smile.

Alfie's tail was wagging furiously, but the boy made no move to put the dog down, he turned n smiled to his friends. John knew they were in trouble, and he started to get angry. He detested unrespectful kids.

"look lad, we don't want any trouble, just give us our dog and we will be on our way" growled John.

"what's with the attitude mate, we found your dog and you don't sound all that fucking grateful" said Danny, holding Alfie tight under his left arm. Alfie still wagging his tail but having a little wriggle every few seconds to try and break free.

"You didn't find my dog boy, I was right behind him and I would have retrieved him no bother on my own, so stop playing silly buggers n drop my dog" remarked John, feeling worried now, there was no one else around, it seemed that everyone had indeed already left the park.

Tina he could tell was getting scared and he couldn't have that, but at the same time he too was feeling a little scared, he knew he wasn't a young man and couldn't possibly win in a show down with not just 1 teenager, but 5 of them. He just hoped that he sounded firm and they would comply with his demand.

"So, you want me to drop your dog mate, are you sure about that?" smirked Danny giving a little laugh.

His friends knew exactly what was going on in their friend's warped mind, they knew when he was about to do something bad...and they liked it.

The group thought nothing of harming any living creature, didn't matter how cute or friendly the animal was, cats were usually the easiest, some were super friendly, they would pet them and play with them for a while before starting to torture them. The best thing the group thought they did was put a small black cat they found in a plastic bag, tie it shut and throw it in a burn. They would then take bets on how long it took the animal to die. This wee black cat took over an hour to succumb to its demise, yowling and frantically trying to escape the rapidly filling bag of water, they took great pleasure in watching the green ASDA bag coming to life as a variety of shapes poked against its surface as the animal fought against its restraint.

 they all started to giggle in anticipation of the fun that was about to begin.

Tina was wringing her hands standing slightly behind her husband, her eyes were brimming with tears, she couldn't believe how things had turned so bad so quickly, nothing bad had happened, but the threat of it was heavy in the air. She just wanted to go home.

John knew his wife was coming close to falling apart emotionally, he didn't want this situation to go on longer than necessary, especially now that the park was so quiet with nobody to call on to help them if things did escalate out of control.

He decided to try and change tactics.

"look lad, I'm sorry, it's just been a long day, I'm very grateful you managed to catch my wee dog. We just want to go home now, so please son, just drop my dog and we will leave, ok" implored John

Danny took two steps over to the low wall of the bridge and sat down. He placed Alfie on his knee and stroked him as the dog licked the boys chin.

"ok mate, seeing as you asked all nice, I will drop your dog" said Danny, with a huge smile he stood up, lifted Alfie up with his hands under the dogs front legs and dropped him over the edge of the bridge.

Time seemed to stand still for John and Tina. They could not comprehend what had just happened, Tina's hand flew to her mouth as she scrunched her eyes closed. John just stood there, slack jawed and staring. The group of teens all stood grinning.

A long wail broke through the silence. Tina staggered backwards, the wail was coming from her, John still stood in shock, trying desperately to understand what had just happened. Finally the sound of his wife's anguish filled wailing broke through the fugue of his uncomprehending mind, he turned and grabbed her by the shoulders, pulling her into his chest, he wrapped his arms tightly around her., as she sobbed into his shirt.

"Holy fuck Danny, that was fucking epic" cried Neil, bouncing about on the spot in sick excitement at what Danny had done, the two girls Hannah and Gwen, although initially looking shocked, were now laughing along with Danny and Neil. Only Dylan looked upset at what had happened. He took a few steps to the bridge wall and looked over the edge.

"for fuck's sake Dan, no need mate, I could have sold that wee dug to somebody" said Dylan, peering down into the gloom trying to see where the dog had landed, with the diminishing light as well as all the bushes and trees, it made it difficult to see anything.

The drop must be roughly 30 feet, there was a small stream at the bottom, plus lots of different colours and sizes of rocks and boulders down there too, he couldn't see Alfie.

Danny was about to reply to Dylan's remark when a high pitch intense yelping seemed to cut through the evening air like nails on chalkboard.

"Oh my God, the wee fuckers still alive" exclaimed Danny, turning to look over the edge beside where his friend stood, the girls and Neil ran over to the edge also, all peering over, to see if they could spot the poor injured animal through the ever darkening shadows.

John and Tina were still standing wrapped in each others arms, when the sudden cries from their little Alfie broke through their shocked grief and sparked them into action.

"Ohhh John, he is still alive" cried Tina, breaking out of John's embrace, she ran past where the teenagers were looking over the edge, she ran to where she knew she would get a better, bigger area to look at the scene below. She had gone to just over the half way point of the bridge, heading back up towards the Abbey where they had first entered the park. After a few moments, her husband had joined her in looking over the edge of the historic bridge, both frantically searching with their desperate eyes to try and locate Alfie.

Suddenly John gripped her wrist.

"there, I see him" he whispered, John pointed to an area of brief movement going under the archway, then it disappeared. He turned to his wife and said in a low voice.

"Tina, try and remain calm love, we will take the path just up there" he nodded to a small entrance a few yards towards the Abbey, which he knew led down to where he was sure he had spotted their dog.

"we have to go get Alfie and get him help, I am sure these little inbred bastards have had their fun, they will leave us alone now, Alfie's crying will bring attention they won't want" John looked into his wife's eyes to make sure she understood, Tina looked at him with tears streaming down her face and sucking in her bottom lip she gave a quick nod of agreement.

John took his wife by the hand and they quickly half walked half jogged up to the entrance of the path that led down to underneath the bridge.

 The group of teens had yet to notice the couple were moving away from them, so intent were they on trying to see where poor Alfie had landed, he had stopped crying now. Down below was silent apart from the soft trickling sound of the shallow stream as it passed over the rocks and stones.

Tina still couldn't believe how horrifically awful the evening had turned, she felt like she had entered a nightmare, none of this can possibly be real she thought, things like this happen to other people in other towns, not here, not us. She was also aware that Alfie was now quiet, too quiet. How could he have survived that fall, did he land on a tree that somehow broke his fall, was he ok and just scared, or, had he actually died after sustaining too great an injury, her brain was bombarding her with so many devastating scenarios she could think of nothing else. She had to get to Alfie, she had to get him safe and away from here.

John could barely see making his way down the steep uneven path, it was very rustic. Steps, where there were any at all, were made up of different sized boulders, which were very hard to navigate, in what was now, the lower they went, almost complete darkness, any light that was left in the disappearing sun, was not permitted access by the many trees which made up their decent towards Alfie.

 The rest of the terrain was bare dirt, made up of varying sizes of twigs, leaves and ferns, which were it seemed, trying to trip them up every few steps. Even though there had been no rain in weeks, the air held a strong cloying smell of damp and decay.

John held his wife's hand tightly to try and protect her from falling, pushing against her arm slightly to act as an anchor and also a brake because she wanted to go faster, the gradient would not allow speed, especially because of their legs not being used to this kind of stress on their muscles, as well as their age.

He caught faint glimpses of the teenagers through the trees as they both made their way down. The young group were still on the bridge, still trying to see his dog, they were setting fire to various bits of rubbish over the edge of the bridge, thankfully the flames extinguished before it was able to reach the bottom, leaving little orange sparks floating and then vanishing.

Like Tina, he just wanted to get Alfie, no matter how hurt he was, just get him safe and away from here. As soon as he achieved that, he was going straight to the police. What was wrong with the youth of today? A good hiding from their parents was lacking he thought, lack of respect for your elders was becoming an epidemic these days, a smack never did him any harm when he was young.

But John knew these kids were beyond that. They had obviously been dragged up and allowed to do whatever they wanted without any repercussions, coddled and spoiled or abused and ignored, he didn't care. Cruel vicious behaviour to a helpless little dog was a red flag to knowing what these kids were like.

Although it seemed much longer, it only took John and Tina a few minutes to reach the bottom of the path, and the ground at their feet evened out to flat terrain.

John and Tina no longer had quite as much cover from the trees now, and even though it was very dark, their faces could be seen, and Tina's light blue cardigan was like a beacon to the group still on the bridge. There was no way of hiding their presence, no other way of getting to Alfie without being seen.

"Oi, old bastard, your dog's dead mate, what are you going down there for" laughed   Neil, shouting and pointing, the rest of the group finding his comment hysterical, all except Danny, who was just staring down at them totally expressionless. Looking up, John found this more horrifying than the rest of the group's laughter. There was something very unsettling with that boy, and it made John very anxious and nervous.

"How can you be so bloody evil, your parents should be ashamed of each and every one of you. I am calling the police on what you have done, you won't be laughing then" sobbed Tina, looking up, crying with more anger, now that the initial shock had worn off, also with the hope that Alfie could be ok.

"shhhh Tina", John advised his wife, suddenly very aware they were not safe yet, he didn't like the feeling he was getting coming from that Danny lad. He thought at that moment that he could feel real malicious intent just by looking at the boy's face. It was like there was no compassion at all, no humanity. It gave him chills. He whispered to his wife.

"love, please, let's find the dog and get out of here, don't talk to them, just ignore them please. We need to get out of here, we will go down towards the bottom gates, no way are we going back up that path towards that lot, I am praying they just leave us now"

Tina looked into her husband's eyes and was unsettled to see fear looking back at her. John was a proud man, he was protective and nothing really fazed him at all. It was sobering to see this unfamiliar emotional in her strong husbands eyes, so she grasped his hand and squeezed, trying to give him a reassuring smile as she agreed. she squeezed his hand again and then turned to go and look for Alfie, still gripping John's hand and leading him with her.

But she meant it. As soon as they got out of here and Alfie was safe, she was going to make sure the police did all they could to find and duly punish these evil little shits. She was going to warn everyone via Facebook and to stay away from the Glen in the evening. What caused some people to turn so evil, she thought.

Tina was so mixed with different emotions, pure horror at what they had done to her little Alfie. Anger that they all thought it was funny, like some kind of ok game. Worry about John and the fear she saw in his face, plus her own fear, which was growing by the second.

John and Tina tried to focus on moving forward, each step was done blind as they could barely see the ground beneath them, but they could hear and see the stream, it would give off little flashes like glitter, as the water managed to somehow capture a little of the elusive light as it trickled and danced over the rocks and stones.

Tina felt something wet hit her face, she instantly knew it was spit, even though she couldn't see, she just knew, especially since it was followed by laughing up above her.

She decided not to mention it to John as she knew he would be livid and may do or say something that would cause the teenagers to retaliate, so she took the sleeve of her cardigan and wiped her face, the substance was thick and slimy and made her stomach clench, Tina was thankful she could not see the snot she had wiped off her face.

The laughing and jeering had now ceased from the group on the bridge, John relaxed just a little as he gently pulled on his wife's hand to bring her next to him.

"I will lead the way love, to make sure if any one of us is going to trip, it will be me, its over now, we will get the little fella and get the hell home" he quickly kissed the top of his wife's head and walked in front of her.

John had only taken two steps in front when he spotted Alfie , lying just at the edge of the stream, his back end still in the shallow water. Not moving. John was heartbroken at losing his little friend. Tina on seeing her pet, rapidly spun and turned her back, she couldn't bear to look at him, John could see her shoulders shaking and knew she was breaking her heart. Those little bastards are going to pay for this he thought to himself, how could anyone hurt a defenceless little animal, Alfie was so loving and sweet natured, now gone forever because of mindless evil morons.

John slid on the little embankment, causing a mini avalanche of dry twigs and grit to flow into the shallow water, he steadied himself and slowly took small steps to where his dog lay, his feet suddenly chilled by the water, but he barely noticed. He squatted down beside the still body and lay his hand gently on the dogs shoulder.

"aww lad, I am so sorry this happened to you" said john, suddenly come over with raw emotion as he stroked the familiar soft fur, john gasped twice as fat tears rolled down his cheeks and dripped off his chin, to be carried away in the water of the stream. He got a hold of himself quickly, he needed to be strong for Tina, she needed him more than ever just now.

Just as John tenderly cupped his hand under the dog's ribs and his other under Alfie's rear, Alfie gave a small cry and a single thump of his tail.

John became still, he drew in a quick breath and held it. Had he imagined the small noise, had the tail wag just been a trick of the near non existent light? He was scared to hope for such a miracle.

Alfie confirmed that he was indeed alive with another small tail thump.

"Tina..... oh my God, Tina he is alive, give me your cardigan to wrap him in, he is hurt but I cant tell how bad, we need to get to a bit more light to see, hurry love" he turned to his wife, keeping one hand on the dogs shoulder as he held out the other towards his wife.

Tina immediately turned around and began frantically complying with Johns request, in her haste her sleeves got tangled and seemed to take forever to remove from her body. Finaly free of the garment, she stepped forward and she too stepped into the stream, stumbling on a few slippery rocks, she handed John the cardigan as she steadied herself by placing a hand on her husband's back.

All thoughts of the teenage group gone as they focused all of their attention on their beloved little dog. John carefully tucked the warm cardigan round Alfie's little body, hoping the contact and scent of them would give the dog some comfort and feeling of safety.

John was terrified to actually touch his dog, he had no idea what broken bones there were or if Alfie had any internal bleeding. But touch him he must, he tried to be as gentle as he could, supporting the little body as much as he could as he very slowly scooped him up and brought himself to a standing position, carrying the dog with as much care as a new born baby.

They stood still for a few seconds as Tina tenderly stroked the top of Alfie's head. She could barely see anything, were the dark patches blood or just dirt, there was no way of knowing yet, but she could see two little sparkling eyes blinking at her. That gave her hope, she looked up into her husband's tear filled eyes.

"let's get this little lad straight to the vet, we can deal with all that has happened later" she said rubbing up and down John's arm.

They nodded at each other in confirmation and slowly made their way out of the stream, the embankment was very small, Tina placed her hands on John's back to steady him as he took one large step to get back onto the path, then she herself held onto the waistband of her husband's trousers to pull herself up to join him.

After ensuring that Alfie was as comfortable as possible, they walked at a gentle but hurried pace along the dirt path towards the bottom Glen Gate. Their footwear being waterlogged, were making small squelching noises as they walked, Their eyes had become a little bit accustomed to the darkness, and they knew the path very well, although uneven in places, it should be fine to navigate without hidden obstacles along the way.

"I can't believe all this love, why? Just why did they do this? I never knew kids could be so evil" said John quietly, breaking the silence that they found themselves walking in,

"I don't think some kids have a conscience or an ounce of respect for anything or anyone these days" sniffed Tina, silently crying at the cruelty and anguish that they had endured.

"I've heard of them destroying property, fighting, drinking and causing a nuisance, but I have never heard of anything on this scale love, I just can't get my head around hurting a little dog, I would have preferred they just gave me a good hiding, that I could accept better than this" answered John, glancing down at his dog and gently using his thumb to stroke the little patch of fur under it.

His wife said nothing, she didn't know what to say, she was still in shock at it all, so she placed her hand on the small of John's back as they walked. She hoped the contact was as comforting to John as it was for her.

As they made their way along the winding dirt path, the trees and bushes as well as the steep embankment on either side, gave Tina a feeling of confinement, but also it gave a little comfort too, knowing they were not far from one of the exits from the park. She silently prayed that Alfie was going to be ok, he was very quiet which disturbed her, not knowing if dogs could go into shock, was that the reason he was so quiet, or was it that he now felt safe in Johns arms and knew he was away from the cruelty he had suffered at the hands of those teenagers.

Tina wished more than ever that they had picked a different place to have their evening walk. Limekilns, or along Patties Muir would have been safer. But Tina knew that was just wishful thinking because of what had occurred tonight, was anywhere safe really. With no crystal ball there was no way of knowing how safe any place would be, regardless of how often they had been there without incident, badness can and does happen anywhere.

She wondered what kind of things those kids were capable of. What they had done was horrific and cruel beyond her imagination, but she doubted this was their first time. They had done things like this before, she was sure of it.

Tina always shared missing pet posts on Facebook, sometimes the precious furry family members returned home or were found, but now she began to wonder at the ones that were never found. Had they met a violent end from others like these teenagers tonight, just how many nasty people were out in the world. Tina suddenly realised on a new level that her life was vastly different from others, on account of how she was brought up, and she thanked her lucky stars at the life she had.

She thought of her grandkids, she couldn't imagine any one of them ever acting in such a bad way. It made her sick to her stomach just thinking about it.

The couple knew they were almost at the little waterfall that was ahead of them, which was very close to the play park. they could hear the water as it fell onto the ground below, it was a gentle sound, mainly because there was hardly any water because of the drought that Fife was experiencing, it was almost a musical sound to the ear.

Suddenly John stopped in his tracks and Tina could feel all the muscles in his back tense up. She instantly felt dread at what the reason could be.

"oh John, has he gone" cried Tina, hands flying to her mouth, thinking the worst. That Alfie had died in his master's arms.

John gave no answer, the reason he had stopped walking was evident and was walking towards them.

"So you found your wee dog then mate" sneered the lad called Dylan. The rest of the group all coming into focus the closer they got to John and Tina.

The group had noticed from their viewpoint on the bridge, that the couple had found the dog and were now trying to sneak away by going along one of the lower paths. They had watched in silence as John and Tina had slowly walked away carrying a small blue bundle.

They had contemplated letting them go, but Danny had said that the couple were disrespecting them, being sneaky and he didn't like the way that the old bastard had spoke to him earlier, he didn't think that they should let the couple away with that.

So they had decided to cut off their exit by running past the museum and hothouse and taking the steps and path just past the buildings, they crossed the small metal bridge where they planned to meet the couple as they were walking towards the playpark, which was very close to the gates which led onto the street lit safety of Netherton Broad street.

John, began to feel overwhelmed, he felt terrified that the nightmare was continuing, he felt fear for his wife, concern for Alfie, plus the immense feeling of frustration at being so damn close to freedom and being able to see the faint orange glow from the street lamps in the near distance which gave the promise of other people and much needed help. So damn close.

"NO, I will not put up with your fucking terrorising a minute longer, you bunch of evil little bastards, now bugger off and leave us alone, you've already done your damage" John shouted at the group, spitting saliva as his temper erupted.

John was the type of person that lashed out when fear rose up in him. He couldn't help it, it was just the way he was, he didn't know why he reacted the way he did in certain situations. It was just a reflex of his persona he couldn't control. Strangers sometimes found him too aggressive, he was far from it, he was in reality a big softy, his friends and family understood it was just his way of coping, albeit badly.

Tina stood there wide eyed and trembling, now gripping onto her husbands arm with both hands, at a loss of what to do or say, her heart hammering against her ribs and nausea caused by fear gathering in the pit of her stomach.

Suddenly there was a very fast blur of movement followed by a loud crack of sound. Initially Tina had no idea what it was, but then Johns arm was violently ripped from her grasp as her husband fell backwards onto the path, because she had been gripping her husbands arm so tightly, she too lost her balance and also fell backwards, but twisted a little as she fell and landed on her left hip, with her elbow breaking the hard fall. A sharp stabbing pain immediately ran up her arm which took her breath away, she looked to her left to check on John and was horrified at what she could see in the shadows.

John was lying on his back, arms flung out to the side, his head was facing towards her and was covered in a black oozing liquid flowing from his nose, it was making fast flowing rivers down the side of his face, dripping from his cheek and mixing with the dirt on the ground.

Tina knew it was blood, there was no true colour because of the lack of light, but she knew exactly what it was. John was unconscious, knocked out by the vicious punch from Danny, she didn't even see it coming, and she very much doubted that John had either.

Lying at the side of John's body was little Alfie, still partly wrapped in her cardigan, he was trying to crawl and was whimpering. Tina opened her mouth and started to scream.

"shut the fuck up bitch" snarled Danny as he bent and gave the distressed woman a hard slap on the face, she had barely enough time to make much of a noise before the shock and sting of the slap had rendered her mute, with her hand now on her cheek, she sat there staring up at him with huge terrified eyes.

Danny knew the woman was absolutely petrified, she would be easy to control, he loved the feeling of terror he felt when he inflicted it on others, and he did it so well. He knew his friends were all scared of him, he didn't care as long as people did what he said and agreed with anything he suggested.

Danny could see the shape on the ground trying to move, as well as the pitiful whimpers that the dog was giving with every little bit of effort it made in an attempt to crawl away.

Hannah and Gwen had moved over to where Alfie lay, they were bent over the animal trying to entangle it from the cloth that was still wrapped around it's hind quarters. Neil and Dylan had walked past and behind where John and Tina were lying on the ground, so even if they wanted to, they definitely couldn't escape.

"it's crazy how this wee shit is still breathing" remarked Gwen as she yanked the cardigan from under the hurt dog, causing it to yelp out in pain.

"not for much longer though, thing's near dead, can't even stand up for fuck's sake, they should have just left the wee cunt" smirked Danny as he turned and looked down at Tina with utter disgust. His fists still clenched, he looked malicious and unpredictable.

He turned from where Tina and an unconscious John lay and stepped over to where the little dog was lying and nudged it with his foot, which caused Alfie to cry out again.

"Please son, please leave him alone, we need to get him to a vet, I won't tell him or anyone else what happened, I promise you, please for the love of God just leave us alone, we don't want any trouble" sobbed Tina, openly crying with glistening snot dripping from her nose, her cheek had started to swell and felt numb, she reached out her hands in a begging gesture towards Danny then clasped them in front of her against her chest as she looked up into the boy's face, pleading him with her eyes.

John had started to give out a low moan. He had bent his knees up towards his rear end and was trying to turn onto his side.

Tina feeling relief that he was coming around, scooted over to be closer to him so she could help him as he came to, she continually kept glancing at Danny, scared he was going to nudge Alfie again.

Hannah and Gwen were no longer hunched over Alfie, they were each lighting cigarettes and sitting on an old rotten tree log at the edge of the path, the tip of the cigarettes glowing red in the darkness every time they took a drag, the girls appeared bored with what was going on and were talking quietly with each other. Although Tina did not look behind her, she knew the other two boys were still there, she could hear the small pieces of gravel on the path crunch and scrape when the boys shifted their footing

"Are you for fucking real, no vet can save that mess" said Danny, looking down at the still dog, snorting in deep through his nose, clearing his throat and then spitting phlegm onto it's fur.

"I think the kindest thing to do would be to put the little fucker out it's misery, save you a few bob in vet bills too" he said as he crouched down and straddled the shitzu's small body. He tenderly stroked the head and body of Alfie in slow gentle sweeps.

John was now sitting on the ground beside his wife, disorientated and extremely dizzy, still feeling the effects of the punch which had knocked him unconscious. His nose was no longer bleeding, the blood now drying and was turning crusty on his cheeks. Tina had one arm wrapped around his broad shoulders and the other hand was resting on his thigh, she felt like she was being torn in two, she had to protect Alfie, but she also had to make sure her husband was ok too.

She was being forced to be the strong one in a situation that was well out of her depth, john was the one who would deal with conflict issues, not her, she had no idea how to handle this event, her reasonable thinking was shutting down, her mind refusing to deal with what was now her responsibility to sort out with John being out of action to do so. Her mouth opened and shut like a goldfish as she struggled with her inner conflict.

Danny was now staring at her as he remained straddled over Alfie, no expression at all on his face that she could see in the gloom. She looked at her husband, his eyes were half open and he was blinking slowly and frowning, he was trying so hard to remove the fog from his head. she turned her attention back to Danny and just shook her head.

Danny stood up from his crouched position with the dog now positioned between his feet, Tina felt pure and complete dread as he lifted his foot and brought it back down with immense force onto Alfie ribcage.

There was a sickening crunching noise that sounded much louder than it actually was, which was followed by a series of pitiful heart breaking yelps that filled the night air. The group of friends all started laughing at the animal's pain and distress, the girls that were sitting on the log had stood up and were rushing over, coming for a closer look at the distressed dog.

Hannah having almost finished her cigarette, bent over the little body, giggling as she stubbed it out on the dogs head, sending orange sparks cascading all around where Alfie was lying. The dog made no sound but gave a long shudder and was still.

"holy fuck man, that was sick" said Neil as he bounced on the balls of his feet in obvious glee at what Danny had just done, laughing and enjoying it even more when Hannah had stubbed her cigarette out, right on the dogs head, he had not expected her to do that, he thought girls were meant to be too soft and mushy to do things like that.

"jeez, that fucking stinks, I think you have cooked the wee fuckers brain Hannah" sniffed Gwen as she covered her nose with the sleeve of her hoody in a futile attempt to prevent the rancid smell of burnt fur and skin, which hung heavy in the still air from reaching her nostrils.

"NO" Tina wailed as she started to crawl to Alfie, his pitiful cries had made Tina move immediately, she stood up and stumbled towards her dog. before she could reach him, Danny grabbed her arm and yanked her backwards, she turned and running on adrenaline slapped him hard across his face. Danny let her arm go, he couldn't believe she had hit him. Just as Tina reached the injured dog, and crouched beside him, she felt herself flying onto her right side and all the air left her lungs.

The rage in Danny was immediate and violent. How dare that old fucking cow slap him. He took one step towards her and kicked her hard in the side of her abdomen with all the force he could muster, he then began stomping on her legs, rapidly three times.

"who the fuck do you think you are you old bitch, no cunt get's to touch me without fucking regretting it" shrieked Danny bending over the curled up form of Tina, she was finding it difficult to breathe, her stomach was going into spasm, she managed to turn her head before she vomited bile onto the dirt beside her, she kept retching even though there was nothing more to come out. A string of gelatinous snot hung from her nose and mixed in with the trail of thick mucus that was coming from her mouth, she was gasping for breath and finally managed to draw a long groaning breath into her empty oxygen starved lungs.

Tina was beyond petrified, pain like she had never experienced before was exploding all over her body. Alfie was momentarily forgotten She was aware that the boy had kicked her fiercely with a lot of force and had knocked all the wind out her, she barely felt the pain in her legs at first but now they were agony and felt like they were on fire. Her head felt like it was being hit with a sledgehammer every time she retched.

 Her lungs struggled for air, she felt sure they were folding in on themselves. After a few gasping breaths the pain seemed to intensify if that was even possible. That Danny boy was bent over her, spittle dropping onto her exposed cheek as he roared in her face. She kept herself rolled in a ball, scared to move in case he hurt her again. Dirt and leaves stuck to her other cheek, her snot and mucus acting as a glue from where her face had touched the ground.

She didn't know exactly how long she lay curled in a ball while the boy stood over her, with her eyes closed so tightly her mind refused any cognitive function. Tina felt rather than saw Danny move away from her, she slowly opened her eyes.

The boy who had just assaulted her was now calmly lighting a cigarette, the flame from the lighter burning bright as it kissed the end of the cigarette to life. He was standing beside his two male companions speaking in hushed tones, they stood just a few feet behind her husband.

John was staring in her direction. In the darkness she couldn't make out if he was staring at her or where Alfie lay.

ALFIE, Tina spun her head in the direction of her dog. she knew he was dead, his small body had already endured immense trauma after Danny had dropped him over the bridge, but after hearing his ribs break and seeing the force in which it was done she was not delusional, no wishful thinking this time. No more happy greetings when they returned after shopping trips, no more morning kisses or cosy cuddles with Alfie on her lap.... Her Alfie was gone.

But she still had to check. Slowly she got herself into an upright position, wiping the leaves and dirt from her face she glanced around. The two girls were back sitting on the rotten log and whispering as they sat close to one another, the boys were still standing behind John, occasionally laughing about something as they carried on their quiet conversation. Her poor husband was sitting with his head down and his hands on either side of his forehead.

Tina knew her husband was broken, she knew it had affected him deeply not being able to protect her and Alfie. He couldn't. She accepted he had no chance of carrying out his duty of care towards them, but John thought differently, this she knew only to well, he would see himself as a failure regardless of how impossible the situation was.

Tina very slowly crawled on her hands and knees towards the still body of her dog, the girls glanced her way but then ignored her as they carried on chatting, she couldn't see what the boy's or her husband were doing as they were now behind her, she felt the grit digging into her palms as she made her way forward, she welcomed the discomfort of it but didn't know why.

Tina having reached Alfie looked down at her beloved pet, fat tears dripping from her chin, she gently laid a hand on the dog's shoulder. No movement, she hadn't expected there to be.

Tina gently took her cardigan which was lying beside Alfie and laid it over him, she didn't want to see the damage to his small frame, no way could she take visually seeing the damage he had had inflicted on him. She was thankful for the darkness.

Covering his entire body with the garment, she gently tucked the edges under his legs and head, still trying not to cause him pain even though he was gone.

At a loss of what to do, and feeling sudden immense separation, Tina stood up.

On pain filled legs and clutching her side she slowly limped over to her husband and sat down beside him. The boys momentarily stopped talking and watched her as she lowered herself to be beside John, after a few seconds she could hear them talking again, but she also heard them moving a little further away up the path. Were they getting bored, had the evil game now ended because Alfie was dead.

Tina laid a hand gingerly on John's forearm, he turned towards her and looked at her with such loss and pain as he put his big strong callused hand on top of hers.

"love, I am so so very sorry" he gasped at her, emotion cutting off his speech as he drew in a quick shuddering breath.

Tina tried her best to give him a reassuring smile, her bottom lip was trembling so bad, she hoped John couldn't see it in the gloom. She gently took his hand and kissed his knuckles and whispered to him.

"we are going to get through this, it cant go on forever, none of this is in any way your fault John, we are completely powerless with these kids, keep strong, we will do whatever they want, we wont fight n hopefully it will be all over soon ok"

John nodded his response and they clung to one another as they sat in the dirt, each feeling the others pain and anguish, silently praying it would be over soon and trying to ignore the physical pain of their own injuries. Thoughts of escape no longer had any place in their minds, they knew it was futile, they were completely and utterly at the disposal of these teenagers, playthings in every sense of the word.

As he sat there on that dirt path. John wondered if he had missed anything in the local news. He knew that the bus station especially was having some issues with certain youths, but not on this scale, just who were these kids.

If he was completely honest with himself, he knew that because any news of antisocial behaviour was not something that had affected him or his friends and family, then it didn't really get to him on a personal level, he would more than likely just scan and skip any relevant news of violent bratty kids. They were someone else's problem. But not now, now it was his problem, he felt ashamed that he hadn't paid more attention to out of control kids in his hometown and how it was affecting people like him and his wife. He remembered an old saying which rang true 'it takes a village to raise a child' but society now demands that you mind your own business. Growing up as a child himself he had a lot of respect for adults, if he was caught doing anything on toward, he would get reprimanded by any adult who caught him, n god forbid that adult knew your parents, coz that would mean another clip round the ear when you got home. He wondered when it had all started to go wrong.

Tina was thinking of her family, what had happened tonight was going to shock and disgust them. They had no way of knowing the horror their parents were enduring and for that Tina was thankful. She didn't like the way her thought process was going, she wondered if she would even see them again, they had thought nothing of killing a little defenceless dog, were they the type that would try and cover what they had done by also murdering John and herself, it was their grandson Jack's birthday tomorrow, would they be around to celebrate anymore family events?

Tina gave an involuntary shudder of fear. She had to make herself stop thinking that way, she told herself that everything was going to be ok, this was all a nightmare. You wake up from nightmares.

She lent in even closer to her husband, it was true he couldn't protect her, he couldn't shield her from any harm these kids decided to inflict on her, but the warmth of his body, the sound of his breathing and his very presence gave her huge comfort.

Multiple heavy scuffing footsteps came up behind the helpless couple. John and Tina kept their eyes in front, fear locking their bruised bodies from moving a muscle as the steps got closer. Tina closed her eyes and gripped her husband's hand tightly, John gripped hers back just as firm, waiting on a blow, a shove or even a kick or slap.

The three boys walked towards and past John and Tina, they didn't even look at them. They stopped in front of the two girls that were still seated on the log.

The couple could hear mumbled words but couldn't make anything out as to what they were saying. After a couple of minutes, the girls stood and followed behind Danny, Dylan and Neil who were walking away from their victims and strolling along towards the bottom playpark near the bottom Glen gates, the young group didn't even look back. John and Tina were terrified to hope, but within a few more minutes the group had disappeared from view, their footsteps could no longer be heard. The night had turned silent.

Still john and Tina sat there, too terrified to move, in disbelief that the teens had left. The nightmare was over.

John, who had now almost recovered from his sickening punch from Danny, and feeling his resolve returning, turned to his wife and whispered close to her ear.

"Tina love, can you walk, I didn't see what these bastards did to you but I know they hurt you, I know they killed Alfie, but we have to go, they may come back, the car's not far, it cant be that late, the first person we see we will ask for help"

Tina looking up into her husband's face, she could see his eyes glistening as he looked at her, and although she couldn't make his features out properly, she could see a large swelling around his cheek and lip on the outline of his face, it was distorted and fat and did not resemble the features she knew as well as her own. They both needed medical attention, but priority for now was getting out of this park.

She gave a brief nod and slowly they both began to stand. John was up first and realised he still felt a bit dizzy as he staggered a few steps backwards, almost falling before he regained his footing and balance. He helped his wife stand, which was a bit slower than himself, by gently gripping her arm with his right hand and then sliding his left under her armpit. He eased her up. Tina gave a small groan of pain as she returned to an upright position, the pain in her ribs far stronger than the ache in her legs, she wondered if Danny had broken a few of her bones when he had kicked her so violently.

After they had caught their breath with the exertion of just standing, they turned their attention to Alfie.

Silently they stepped over to the small body, john bent down and very gently scooped him up, just like he did when they had first found him injured under the bridge. As he lovingly cradled their little companion, john and Tina silently turned and started walking back along the path from the direction they had first came.

Progress immediately was very slow, Tina was in too much pain to go any faster, the muscles in her legs ached so bad with every step, every time she put weight on either injured leg she felt like Danny was kicking her all over again, plus it really hurt to breath and even very small movements caused her to experience sharp stabbing pain in the side where that boy had initially started his assault when she had gone to protect Alfie.

John stopped walking, he stood for a few seconds and took in his surroundings, looking to his left and right, he seemed to be looking for something.

"why have we stopped" breathed Tina.

"Sweetheart, we are going to leave this little lad somewhere safe, we will come back for him I promise. I need to help you, we have to get out this park and you are struggling so much, you need my help"

"oh John no, we can't, we need to take him home with us, I'm not leaving him here"

Tina's tears had started afresh, which was agony to watch for John, he didn't want to leave the dog, but they were getting nowhere fast at this rate. He hated having to do it.

He stepped away from the path by taking 3 large strides up the steep banking that was on either side of the path. There he chose a medium sized bush to lay Alfie behind, he then gathered handfuls of leaves and twigs, and placed the decaying musty smelling debris up around and over the temporary resting place, hoping to camouflage the area because of the light blue in his wife's cardigan.

Tina knew her husband was right, she knew she was slowing any progress they hoped to make, but at this time she hated John. She hated that he was right.

Hoping that he had covered the area enough, John half slid back down to where his wife was standing, bringing a little avalanche to follow his descent of the same material he had scooped in his hands to semi bury their dog.

"we know where he is love, he won't be there for long" said John tenderly as he kissed her on the top of her head".

John felt Tina tense and she recoiled from his touch, he didn't blame her, he hated himself right now too.

But what choice did he have, as much as he loved that little ball of fur, Alfie was gone, but they were still here, and he had to now get his wife to safety and get her some much needed medical assistance. It was obvious to John that Tina had broken a rib, maybe more than one. John knew how painful that was, he himself had broken two ribs when he had fallen out of the loft.

Tina had sent him up there to start bringing down the Christmas tree and all the seasonal decorations a few years ago. He had passed her down almost all the boxes, but it was the second last box of Christmas crap that made him fall.

As he had passed the box down to Tina, he was bending through the hatch when a spider of Jurassic proportions had crawled out a little gap where the dried out brown packaging tape hadn't quite sealed the box. Knowing Tina would kill him if he handed her her personal phobia albeit accidentally , he had tried to quickly grab the offending arachnid, in his haste he had lost his balance and fell straight through the hatch, banging his ribs on the wooden ramsay ladder as he fell.

Tina had started limping back along the path. John knew that she didn't really hold it against him having to leave Alfie. It was just her grief, anger and frustration being directed onto himself. He knew that his wife just needed a few minutes to process her feelings and then she would accept what they had had to do for their own wellbeing given the terrible circumstances.

John followed behind his heartbroken wife and after a few steps he offered the support of his arm by crooking his elbow towards her to link with her own to ease her walking, but Tina immediately grimaced in pain as she accepted the offered support, she took a hissing breath in through her clenched teeth.

"I can't John, I feel like a sharp stick is digging in me when I put pressure on that arm, I think it's pulling the muscles in my side, I think my ribs are broken" she panted.

"perhaps if I go to the other side it won't be as painful, and just put your hand in mine, I'm a lot taller than you n I think your reaching too much because of it" offered John as he stepped round to her other side, crooking his arm but keeping his elbow tight at his side, therefor only offering his hand which she could use for support.

But even that proved too painful. John was at a loss, feeling useless and unable to ease his wife's obvious discomfort he didn't know what to do for the best.

He thought about suggesting that she remain here while he went for help, but he knew Tina would never allow that. She was scared and in immense pain, emotionally as well as physically. He felt overwhelmed with frustration. He followed along beside her, ensuring that the path ahead was clear and being ready to help her if she needed him.

The couple continued to limp slowly along the winding dirt path, stopping every few feet just so Tina could catch her breath. They heard a rustle in nearby foliage but could not see what had caused it, rabbit, squirrel, rat or some other small creature out foraging in the undergrowth no doubt. Their vision was just shadows and shapes in the darkness of the night as they plodded along.

Eventually they were almost at the little foot bridge that went over the near dried up stream that ran under and was very close to the double bridge where this nightmare had all started. They could see the welcome yellow glow from the ornamental lamps that were on the main walkway over the ancient bridge and which led up to the Abbey.

"Thank God" Tina sobbed. Suddenly her legs went out from under her and she collapsed to the ground, crying out in agony as she did so.

John had tried to grab her as she fell but she slipped like butter through his fingers. He watched helplessly as she seemed to melt down onto the dirt.

John threw himself onto the path beside her, eyes wide with fear and concern, suddenly terrified that she had more damage inside than just a few broken ribs, he was scared that she may have some internal bleeding somewhere, what is her kidneys were damaged, what if her liver was torn and bleeding, were her bowels ripped and poisoning her slowly from the inside. It was amazing how the human mind under stress could produce so many reasons for her collapse in what was in reality, just a couple of seconds.

"oh my God, Tina, TINA, love what is it, please" gasped John as he placed his hands on either side of his wife's head, his face so close to her own, desperately trying to read her expression, his knees not even feeling the sharp sting of the grit and gravel that was cutting through the thin material of his trousers, poking into his skin as the pressure of his knees in contact with the earth was stronger because his toes were bent at an angle forcing the heels of his feet into his buttocks as he bent over his wife.

Tina had fainted, she was unresponsive, but she was breathing. It's just the pain, John told himself, she is ok, people pass out from pain all the time. He nodded into the darkness as he gently stroked his wife's head. his eyes brimmed with tears but he blinked them back, it was distorting his already compromised vision in such little light.

"For fucks sake man, get a bloody grip" he told himself as he stood up and frantically looked around him.

He lifted his arms and ran his fingers through his hair, violently gripping handfuls on either side of his head as he spun round, desperately looking for aid in the gloom and finding nothing but trees and damn bushes. Again' he contemplated leaving her and making his way out the park to bring back help. He felt fit enough, he was no longer dizzy and disorientated from that knockout punch, his face felt hot, fat and painful but that was the full extent of his injuries.

John knelt back down beside his wife and placed a soft kiss onto her forehead. He tasted the salty sweat that was covering her brow, much more moisture than was on his own.

He fully realised at that moment just how much excruciating pain she must have been in. he looked as hard as he could at her face. Even in the grey and black world that he was living in, he could see glistening patches where the dim light touched her skin, there was even a little pool of moisture in the little hollow of her neck in between her collar bones.

He had made up his mind, Tina needed help and she needed it now.

Leaving his wife lying there all alone on that path was probably the hardest decision John felt he had ever made. He felt like he was being torn in half as he started to walk away from the most important person in his life. It hit him like a freight train just how much he loved and adored his wife, yes, they fought, they didn't agree on everything, they had had some hard times over the years, but they were inseparable and would gladly die for each other.

John had barely started walking up the steep path full of boulders. The same path they had both ventured down when they had spotted Alfie from their viewpoint on the double bridge, when he heard Tina calling out to him.

"JOHN"

He could hear the panic in her voice, and it cut through his heart like a razor blade. He immediately turned and called out to her.

"Tina love, I'm right here"

John could hear her starting to hyperventilate. He could slap himself for not realising what waking up alone and abandoned would do to her. Why the Hell didn't he think before leaving her.

He half stumbled and half jogged in the few measly seconds it took him to reach where he could make out the shape of his wife. Tina was sobbing, the sound of it making John wish in that moment that he was deaf, it hurt him on a scale he wouldn't have thought possible, listening to her cries felt like she was voicing his betrayal.

Tina, upon waking, realised she couldn't see or hear John. It hit her straight away that she was alone. Adrenaline from fear and panic had made Tina forget about the pain she was in. she had gotten up and threw herself into a kneeling position before the agony resurfaced and stopped her from doing anything else. She sat on her legs and wrapped her arms around herself as her eyes darted from left to right. The feeling of solitude was absolute. She had cried out for her husband and relief that was immense enveloped her as her husband immediately answered her call. She sobbed in gratitude. Now able to see the familiar shape of her husband hurrying towards her after hearing him call back to her.

Without a word, John got on the ground beside his wife and wrapped his arms around her small shuddering shoulders, quickly lessening his hold when Tina gasped in pain.

"love I'm sorry, I was just trying to get help, I panicked when you fainted, I didn't know what to do, please forgive me, I will never leave you like that again" implored John as he sat there now rubbing both Tina's arms with his hands in vigorous long strokes.

"stop doing that John, it hurts like hell" snapped Tina

"sorry" replied John as he hung his head and let his arms fall down to his side.

Tina felt guilty for snapping at him, she knew he was struggling with all that had occurred.

She sniffed hard and rubbed her face onto her shoulder to remove the tears that were soaking her skin. Tina then reached out a hand and rubbed John's knee, she smiled at him as he brought his head up to look into her eyes. It was all the reassurance he needed in that moment. He smiled back at her and placed his own, much larger hand on top of hers and gave her a little pat.

"so, does this old bird think she can stand and make it up to the top of that path" smiled John as he gave a slight flick of his head to indicate the path behind him,

Tina returned the smile with fresh tears threatening to fall from her eyes. She squeezed her eyes closed for 3 seconds and upon opening them she gave a strong nod to her husband.

That path was her Everest, she knew it was going to be slow and very painful, but she had to do it. They had to get out this park which was feeling like a prison. They both had no idea how long they had been here, both having lost all sense of time from lapses in consciousness.

John stood up first, brushing off the grit and dirt from his trousers he took both of Tina's hands in his and gently helped ease her up to an almost standing position, being fully erect was too painful for her.

So engrossed were they on each other that they did not notice three familiar figures walking towards them from the opposite end of the path.

"well, well, well, look how far you fuckers managed to come" snarled Danny as he covered the last few feet to stand beside the shocked couple.

Tina on hearing the boy's low growling voice, sank back down on to her knees. The hot stream of her urine quickly spreading through the crotch of her trousers and seeping around her legs causing little rivers to move out and make their way down a slight slope in the path. Tina drew in a hitched breath and began to shake all over. Her fear palpable to all around her. John himself felt the energy and strength vanish from his legs, it was sheer willpower that kept him upright, although he did bend his knees a little before he caught himself from succumbing to his terror.

"holy fuck, she's pissed herself" laughed Dylan, pointing at the terrified woman.

Neil joined in the laughter, both boy's finding it hilarious to see Tina in so much fear and distress. Danny just grinned, hands shoved into his jogging trousers, and even in the bad light, John could see pure evil intent in the boy's eyes. There was nothing there, no humanity at all. John had only seen similar in a nature documentary on National Geographic a few months back, he had found the film about the sharks interesting. Perhaps it was the lack of light that made the boys eyes appear pitch black, just like that great whites.

John glanced down at his wife and was disgusted. Not disgusted because her bladder had released it's contents, he was disgusted that these evil little fucktards had made her feel terror so absolute that she had wet herself in total fear.

John swung for the nearest boy as a primal roar erupted from his throat. He moved at a much quicker speed than a man of his age should be capable of, his rage giving him strength and desire to do serious damage. His clenched fist flew through the air and connected with a sickening cracking sound as it slammed into Danny's temple.

The boy seemed to teeter on his legs then fell back. His head and shoulders disappearing into a patch of stinging nettles, the lower part of his body was lying off centre in the path, and his hands were still in the pockets of his trousers. He didn't have time to react to John's advance, nor did he expect it.

Neil and Dylan instantly ceased laughing, they stood still as statues with their mouths wide open, staring where their comrade had fallen. Nobody had ever knocked Danny out before. The shock of what they classed as an old man being able to do that was startling and sobering to witness.

John was past the point of logical thought, panting heavily he launched himself at the other two boys, but they recovered quickly, and the boy called Dylan shoved John back as he came charging towards them.

As John was pushed back, he staggered backwards a few paces but managed to turn himself around before he stumbled and fell to his knees, the force of the fall ripping his trousers and scraping the skin off what was at least a little protection offered from the scant material. His hands slid painfully along the grit and sharp gravel of the path, the small stones acting like a cheese grater on his palms, grit and dirt getting embedded into the injuries by the force of the fall.

Tina was unable to move, frozen in terror and disbelief, she looked on helplessly as she witnessed John attacking Danny, then utter dread filled her heart at the realisation of what this could bring on them as her husband was pushed hard onto the ground by the other two boys.

John rolled onto his side and ignoring the pain in his knees and hands, he frantically side crawled over to his wife, his feet scraping against the surface of the path, the small pieces of grit acting like ball bearings, slowing his progress as he tried to put distance between himself and the younger males, realisation suddenly dawning on him how dangerous he had made their predicament.

  Having made it over to where his wife was kneeling. John felt his heart was going to explode. What the hell had he been thinking. Real tangible fear gripped him at the very centre of his being. They were so close to the main path and within grasp of their freedom, he knew he had ruined any chance they had of getting away and up to safety now. Scared beyond anything he had ever felt before. He suddenly felt like a little child again.

Neil crouched over the struggling moving body of Danny. The boy was coming around very quickly and had already swore at his friend to get the fuck away from him. Neil complying with the order was now standing a few feet away, although wanting to help his friend, he knew Danny would be filling with up malevolent violence and would think nothing of unleashing some of it on a mate.

Dylan had now moved on slightly away from his friends to now be standing guard behind John, aggression oozing off his presence like an unseen wave. John and Tina could hear his heavy breathing above them. They were too scared to look behind them.

The couple watched in dread as Danny seemed to move in slow motion from the nettles and to an upright position. There he stood for what seemed like hours just staring at them, although they couldn't see the boys features too clearly at all, they could see his eyes glinting in the darkness as he looked at them thru eyelids that were tensed and full of malice.

John felt his bowels clench as he gulped audibly as his mouth filled with water brought on by nauseous fear as Danny slowly walked towards them.

Neil allowed a few steps from Danny before he followed on closely behind the rage filled boy, he didn't want to miss a second of what he knew was coming, but he certainly didn't want to get caught in the cross wires of Danny's rage He felt no remorse or sympathy for what was about to be inflicted on the idiot that had felled Danny so embarrassingly. Neil was aware that more than anything, that was what had induced his friend to seek brutal bloody revenge. He also knew that himself or Dylan better not breath a word of it, because it would surely be the end of them if Danny ever had it mentioned to him.

Danny soon stood in front of john, the boy bent slightly and viciously grabbed the front of John's shirt, pulling skin as he twisted the material in his fist and pulled upwards, in an attempt to get John to stand up.

John's legs failed him, such was his fright. His legs refused to offer any assistance in the upward motion that the boys grip had on him. The boy yanked him violently upwards twice, but john felt like a rag doll in the boys clutches, he felt the hair on his chest being ripped out but felt no pain. Adrenalin coursed through his body but his muscles were paralyzed.

With John's refusal to stand, Danny let go of his shirt and violently kicked him in the centre of his chest with the sole of his adidas trainer sending john flying backwards onto the dirt, johns head smacked painfully onto the ground from the force of the impact, sending flashes of white light into his vision.

John briefly looked up into the canopy of trees with the star filled night sky behind them before the face of Danny blocked out the scene as he towered over him.

The boy grinned down at him as he straddled the older man, before pulling back his right arm and punching John straight on his mouth. Blood instantly pooled at the back of John's throat and he knew he had lost a tooth, then he was hit with another punch on the right side of his face, causing his head to snap to the left, he had no time to register any pain as he was hit again on the left side which sent his head back over to the right.

John did not try to protect himself. His arms lay placid at the side of his body, like useless appendages attached to his upper body, no purpose to them but to act like weights, holding him down as the boy pummelled the flesh and bone of his face.

It was then that john's chest spasmed and he coughed out the blood that was filling his mouth, as well as four of his teeth. They lay there on the path in a sea of dark blood like sinister little icebergs.

Danny stood from straddling his victim, and as he lifted his left leg over the bleeding John, he swung it behind him and placed a kick to the man's shoulder, there was not much force behind it as he was slightly off balance. so he quickly gained better footing, drew the leg back again and kicked john repeatedly over and over in a frenzy of temper into his right side and hip.

John arched his back as the pain from the kicks registered in his body, he had protected his ribs by tucking his arm against his side, he knew more hits would be coming after Danny realised he hadn't injured him hard enough with the first kick to his shoulder.

The agony was white hot and intense. He cried out as the pain intensified, his face screwing up in agony, blood oozed freely out from his damaged and broken mouth.

He coughed again, sending a red coppery smelling sticky mist a few inches into the air. Gasping for breath and rolling from side to side in a futile attempt to ease the pain but finding no relief. John hoped the assault was over.

Straight away John felt all the pain vanish, ignored now by his body, to be replaced by the incredible sudden acute feeling of migraine type pain in his testicles. John retracted his limbs instantly and involuntarily curled into a fetal position, the pain from this new sensation of agony bleeding into his stomach and causing him to retch, he thought his bowels were going to go because of the intense cramping in his gut.

Danny was sweating profusely with the exertion of his fury spent on John, his breath was coming in hard and fast pants, as he unleashed his rage on the prone helpless man.

His final kick, a full force assault on John's unprotected groin was the icing on the cake, the cherry on the top, and bringing Danny to achieving the feelgood factor that only inflicting extreme violence and pain on another could bring him.

It felt good, very good. He loved the feeling of resistance when his feet forcibly connected with flesh, he had no idea why he loved inflicting pain, maybe it was the feeling of control over another, or maybe it was knowing he had the power to cause serious harm.

No matter.

He didn't care, he just loved the feeling of freedom and joy it gave him. It made him feel invincible, powerful, superior to all around him. It made him feel like God.

But the feeling was too fleeting. It only lasted a few seconds before it started to fade away, he thought it was a bit like having a really good orgasm, but much better and much more satisfying. He was always chasing the violence high, like some kind of sick junkie, addicted to the next hit. He couldn't get enough, there was never quite enough of it to scratch the itch, he never felt fully satiated

"fucking Hell mate, ye don't hold back do ye" exclaimed Dylan, a little shocked at the level of violence that Danny had inflicted on the older man. He had involuntarily grabbed his own testicles and sucked in a pained breath when he had witnessed his friend kick with shocking force between the legs of the prone bleeding man

"nah, fuck him, the old fucker deserved it after what he did, bet Hannah and Gwen will be wishing they hadn't fucked off hame after they hear about this" grinned Neil.

But he too was a bit shocked at first, no way was he going to let Danny think otherwise though, and if truth be told, although he was initially thinking Danny was taking it a bit far, he still enjoyed watching it happen.

Neil knew he was more of a follower, he wasn't very tough or good at fighting at all, but he did enjoy being a spectator if anyone was getting a good kicking, he enjoyed watching it unfold in front of him, the sound skin made when it was hit with force, the different sounds that a bone could make as it gave in to too much sudden pressure were a special thrill for him, he knew his love of bones breaking had started when he was just 7 years old.

 He thought back to that day when he was playing with his little plastic toy commandoes in his back garden, the 5 year old pain in the arse next door neighbour had put his chubby little arm through a gap in the fence and had grabbed one of his little green men. Neil had been quick and had managed to grip the young boy's little wrist before he could pull it back through the fencing. He didn't really mean to twist the younger boys arm, but he wanted his toy soldier back, he remembered the boy squealing in a high pitch as there was a sudden, way too loud crack as the small arm had suddenly snapped in two, the arm immediately becoming distorted with a large bulge sticking out from the side of it. He could remember being horrified, but the feeling was quickly replaced with satisfaction and a weird kind of Euphoria that he didn't quite understand at the time.

Neil had gotten away with that by pleading to his parents that he was only playing and was sharing his toy with the little boy, but the boy had pulled back as he was handing him the little green toy soldier. His parents had believed him.

John was sobbing and gasping in agony, his whole body felt like it was burning. Sweat was dripping from his brow to mix in with the blood and dirt on the path. The same sticky moisture coated his back, causing his shirt to stick to him like a second skin.

Through his blurred vision, he could see Tina sitting very still, her eyes staring straight ahead of her and still sitting with her legs tucked under her, on her urine soaked trousers. He immediately knew she was going into shock and he was powerless to help her. He just prayed they would leave her alone and only terrorise him, even though he was in more pain than he had ever been in in his entire life, he would take it if it meant they would leave his beloved wife free from any more harm.

John lay there in his curled up position and willed his pain to subside. He could hear Danny pacing back and forth behind him, every few seconds out of the corner of his peripheral vision, he would catch a glimpse of the boy for a second or two before he commenced with his repetition.

"fucking nettle rash all over my face you cunt" Danny suddenly shouted as he stopped pacing long enough to give John a swift kick into his back, making the older man cry out.

John did nothing but try and take the blow. His body was so sore he didn't really feel any higher a pain sensation, but he cried out anyway. Probably just a reaction to the sensation of the kick.

"look at the state of her for fucks sake, sitting in her own pish and looking like she's watching tv or some fucking thing" deflected Dylan, he was beginning to be slightly uncomfortable with what was happening. He liked a bit of violence, but it was starting to go too far now.

Dylan was more comfortable to just have a bit of fun by punching fuck out of someone and then leaving them lying there. He had thought it fun at first when they had all enjoyed hurting and killing that dog, it was just a stupid wee dog, not even a decent breed like a rottweiler or staffy, it was just a wee ball of useless fluff that looked like one of those pathetic Ewok alien creature things from Star Wars.

Tonight though was turning out to be a lot more violent, and for a much more prolonged period than he was used to or had the stomach for. Plus, those folk were old, he hadn't really been violent to elderly people before, he usually just gave them verbal abuse or intimidated them with threats.

He started to try and think of ways to get away from this situation, but he knew Danny would see right through any excuse for him to leave that he came up with, plus with Danny being so angry he knew he ran a very real risk of Danny turning his temper on himself.

Dylan knew he just had to go along with it and take whatever Danny decided to do. He hoped it was going to finish soon though, he was getting hungry and he had half a pizza still left in the fridge from last night, and he wanted to try and steal a few quid from his wee brothers ceramic dinosaur bank, the little shit having got quite a few notes of cash from his recent 10th birthday.

Danny glanced over to look at Tina but ignored Dylan's remark and turned his attention back down to the defeated crumpled man that lay at his feet. He knew that the man was too terrified to move or say anything, he could feel the fear seeping out of John and he soaked it in like a sponge.

Just as Danny bent forward with his arm outstretched and fingers reaching to grab John by a handful of his hair, there was a sudden blinding light shining down on them, it seemed to light up the whole area, chasing shadows back into the recesses of darkness where the beam of light couldn't reach.

Danny, Neil and Dylan snapped their heads up towards where the offending light was coming from. Neil and Dylan both bringing up an arm to place across their brows, to try and shield their eyes from the painful glare, Neil ducking down as he did so, appearing to think that some object was going to hit him with the sudden appearance of the light.

Only Danny seemed unaffected by the white light from the torch beam, he stared upwards to the top of the path, from his semi bent position. The boy then pulled himself into a fully upright stance and took two steps forward.

Neil immediately took flight, sprinting off along the dirt path away from where his friends stood. He disappeared into the night within seconds.

With the rapid exit from Neil, Dylan too felt his flight response kicking into his limbs as his heart started to race and thump hard against his chest, but the feeling left him after the initial adrenalin rush and he just bobbed his legs where he stood, like a rabbit suddenly caught in headlights and frozen to the spot.

"what the Hell is going on here" shouted a disembodied incredulous voice from behind the light.

Immediately there were numerous figures spilling out from behind the beam of white light, at the same time there were many voices all speaking and shouting orders at once, some further away than others, all moving quickly down the path, appearing black as they crossed across the torch light. In reverse, but still resembling descriptions of near death experiences that some people speak about.

With the many bodies still coming out from behind the light, Danny and Dylan knew they were outnumbered and had no chance of overpowering such a large volume of people. A piercing scream made the two boys jump and then they too, took to their heels and were now making a hasty exit back along the path on which Neil had fled just seconds before.

On seeing the sudden illumination of his surrounding's and hearing the booming voice from above and behind him, John's eyes flew open and wide. He still did not dare to move, he dared not even breath. His body rigid, he could still feel the ominous presence of Danny standing behind him, even though he was no longer there.

Tina, once having the sudden beam of illumination flow across her face, began to scream, long and continuous, the light having slapped her out of the safe recess of her mind that she had closed herself in, she continued to scream as Danny and Dylan ran past her and were gone, then at least four of the shadow figures that were coming towards her, rapidly followed the boys, swallowed by the darkness by this never ending night. There was too much sensory input going on around her for her to cope with, so Tina closed her eyes and continued screaming until someone placed a hand on her shoulder.

Tina's eyes opened and became like saucers as she gazed up into the face of a large muscle laden bald man, her screams ceased but her mouth still grimaced and moved in a silent heart wrenching look of agony and fear. This new strange man gave her a gentle smile as he looked at her with eyes full of concern and kindness, and she instantly knew he meant her no harm. Tina gripped the man by the forearm while his hand lay gently on her shoulder and she sobbed into his skin, using her other hand to grip the front of his t-shirt to try and pull him down and towards her. She was safe, he was here to save her and John.

There were too many people to count now, fleeting figures moving rapidly in many directions, John saw the large man go his wife and was overwhelmed with how gentle he was being with her. He knew by her body language that she was aware the man was there to help.

Someone was talking close to his ear telling him everything was going to be ok, he felt something being laid across his body. John couldn't respond, he lay there struck dumb, the swelling of his mouth and lack of his front teeth making any verbal communication impossible, but thankful for the jacket that someone had placed on him. John slowly turned his head and could see bright flashes of blue and red lights. The whole area was now a hive of activity

A pretty young woman wearing a pink short jumpsuit came to crouch down in front of John, she tenderly stroked the back of his hand with her long fingers, her nails appearing too clean and perfect against Johns filthy, blood encrusted own.

"mister, its ok now, some men that were cutting a shortcut through the park heard what was going on and they ran and called the police from Life night club, we all came down to help and chase them off"

John tried to say thank you, but he just coughed and spat out some blood infused saliva, speckling the young woman's knees with the fluid as he did so, she didn't seem to mind and just kept stroking his hand, too scared of causing any pain by touching him elsewhere.

Bright yellow high visual jackets now made their way down the precarious boulder path towards john and Tina. The ambulance crew went straight to john, knelt on the ground beside him and began assessing his injuries. The pretty young woman had scooted up a bit to give them room. John no longer cared about the pain, he knew he was going to be ok now.

"mmm wfff" he mumbled through his pain filled mouth.

The paramedic thankfully knew what he was trying to say.

"another crew is at your wife sir, lets focus on you, your wife is in excellent hands I promise you, now I know you have had a horrible ordeal, but try and relax as much as possible while we do our checks and we will give you something for the pain, ok sweetheart, you can hold",   the female paramedic briefly stopped talking and looked up at the young woman stroking Johns hand, waiting on the girl giving her name.

"Ebony" the girl answered

"you just hold Ebony's hand and we will work as quickly as we can" she advised as she began to explain that she was going to roll him gently onto his back after feeling round his pelvis, spine and legs.

After the paramedics had finished their checks, john was now strapped in a stretcher with two large orange blocks on either side of his head. at some point he thought he must have passed out because Ebony was no longer stroking his hand and he couldn't see her in the many bodies that were standing in the large crowd that had gathered around him. The ambulance crew had covered him with a light blue waffle type blanket under the straps, tucked between his arms and body which instantly reminded him of poor Alfie. It was the same colour as Tina's cardigan that was used to swaddle the little dog in.

A warm soothing sensation swept over Johns body just a few seconds after feeling a sharp scratch in the crook of his arm, he glanced over in the direction that he thought Tina was in, but he could only move his eyes, the orange blocks effectively preventing him from moving his head. he couldn't see her. But he knew she was safe, he closed his eyes and passed out.

Tina having been assessed quicker than her husband, was now almost at the top of the path, many willing caring hands, helping the ambulance crew take the stretcher up safely, she too was in a stretcher and had also received a strong pethidine painkiller, and although it was making her much more comfortable, she refused to let the paramedics take her up towards the Abbey and the waiting ambulance without her husband coming up at the same time. Thankfully John and his stretcher were just seconds behind her.

The police were trying to move the crowds back to allow the ambulance crews an easy passage, and as she gazed at the faces of onlookers, Tina couldn't help notice the look of horror on their faces, some, mostly females, were even crying, hands covering their mouths as they sobbed into each other or their boyfriends chests. Others stood shaking their heads in disbelief at what they were witnessing.

Tina didn't realise how horrific their injuries were until she saw John.

Now that they were out of the dark and gloom and everything was now so bright, Tina felt her heart stop when she caught a small glimpse of the damage to her beautiful husband's face. She barely would have recognised him if she didn't already know it was her John. His face looked like it had been in a car accident, there was not a part of it that wasn't damaged or swollen. And the blood that coated his skin, so much blood in varying degrees of freshness, some of it bright red and very fresh, and some of it cracked and dry and black looking, but even through the blood she could see the dark patches of severe bruising. He was in a bad way.

The ambulance crews were now pushing them up towards the Abbey, with the crowd that had gathered all following behind them, Every now and then, someone would shout out words of encouragement or comfort Tina felt every bump as they made their way, even though she had strong pain relief it was still jarring to her damaged body. Eventually after what seemed longer than it was they passed through the large iron gates, where even more people had gathered, all trying to get a glimpse of what was going on, the police having stopped anymore people from entering the Glen as soon as they arrived at the scene.

Tina felt like the whole of Dunfermline were witnessing the end of what was the most traumatic night of herself and John's lives.

The ambulances were side by side as the couple were wheeled to the doors.

 John had briefly come around and he and Tina were both informed that although they were going in separate vehicles, they were both bound for Edinburgh Royal Infirmary, Tina stretched out her arm and gently patted where john's hand was at the side of his stretcher.

"see you soon love" Tina said as the legs of Johns stretcher collapsed in on themselves as the crew worked it into the back of the waiting ambulance. Then she too was loaded the same way into her own transport.

A policeman was already waiting for Tina inside the ambulance, he informed her that they would get a statement from John when he was up to it. He made her aware that they had arrested two boys on Priory Lane at the side of Andrew Carnegies birth place, which was close to the bottom area of the park, arrested mainly because one of them was covered in blood and they had just been informed over the radio that a serious assault had taken place and suspects had fled on foot to that direction.

Tina didn't feel as much relief as she thought she would, she felt numb and exhausted, but she wanted justice.

Justice for little Alfie, justice for John and justice for herself and for anyone else that these boys had affected at any time with their despicable violence. Her anger started to simmer as she turned to the policeman and said.

"I'm ready to give my statement"

THE END